To those who have faced scarier foes
than dragons in the fight for love
— DH

For my mother, whose selfless love inspires
me to be open, kind, and loving to others
— SL

little bee books

New York, NY
Text copyright © 2018 by Daniel Haack Illustrations copyright © 2018 by Stevie Lewis
All rights reserved, including the right of reproduction in whole or in part in any form.
Manufactured in China RRD 0122
First Edition 10
ISBN 978-1-4998-0552-9
Library of Congress Cataloging-in-Publication Data is available upon request.
littlebeebooks.com
For information about special discounts on bulk purchases,
please contact Little Bee Books at sales@littlebeebooks.com.

A PROUD PARTNERSHIP BETWEEN

glaad + little bee books

A portion of the proceeds from the sale of this
book will be donated to accelerating
LGBTQ acceptance.

Prince & Knight

words by Daniel Haack
pictures by Stevie Lewis

little bee books

Once upon a time,
in a kingdom far from here,

lived a charming prince
who was handsome and sincere.

His parents knew that soon, it would be time he took the throne.
But with a kingdom so grand, the prince could not rule alone.

So the three of them set out and traveled far and wide,
on a quest to find the prince a kind and worthy bride.

The prince met many ladies
(and he made them all swoon!),

but it was soon clear that
he was singing a different tune.

"Thank you," he told his parents. "I appreciate that you tried,
but I'm looking for something different in a partner by my side."

But while the royals were away,
their land faced quite a scare
from a dragon fast approaching,
breathing fire everywhere!

All the villagers ran in fear!
Even the soldiers hid and fled.
"This vicious beast is far too great.
We must retreat or we'll be dead!"

The prince heard the dreadful news,
and he raced home with all his might.
To protect his precious realm,
the prince was ready for a fight.

Alas! Before you fear our prince
had to face the beast alone . . .

along on horseback
came a knight
cloaked in armor that
brightly shone.

The dragon charged upon our heroes,
thinking it had already won,
but the knight had a bold idea,
and raised his shield to face the sun.

The glare hit the shining metal, blinding the dragon's fiery eyes,
but it was what the prince did next that really caught it by surprise!

The prince had climbed atop the dragon
and tied a rope around its head.

He wrapped the cord around the neck
and down the body like a thread.

The plan had worked! The dragon was caught.
Its body was tied and bound,
but the prince up high had lost his grip
and was falling to the ground!

The knight below jumped on his horse
and they began to race.

The prince was caught and free from harm,
held in the knight's embrace.

"You saved my life!"
"And you saved mine!"
They said to one another.

And on the two men's wedding day,
the air filled with cheer and laughter,
for the prince and his shining knight
would live happily ever after.

"We have finally found someone who is perfect for our boy!"

The knight took off his helmet
to reveal his handsome face,

And in a flash, to each it felt
there simply was no other.

and as they gazed
into each other's eyes,
their hearts
began to race.

As the villagers returned,
it became clear to those around
that the prince's one true love
had at last been surely found.

The king and queen
had come back too,
and were overwhelmed
with joy.